# MY
## *Married*
# BOYFRIEND

Also by Cydney Rax

**The Love & Revenge Series**
*My Married Boyfriend*
*If Your Wife Only Knew*

*My Daughter's Boyfriend*
*My Husband's Girlfriend*
*Scandalous Betrayal*
*My Sister's Ex*
*Brothers & Wives*

*Reckless* (with Niobia Bryant and Grace Octavia)
*Crush* (with Michele Grant and Lutishia Lovely)

**Published by Dafina Books**